I
Witness

Brian's Footsteps

By Carol Gorman
Illustrated by Ed Koehler

CPH™
SAINT LOUIS

Copyright © 1994 by Carol Gorman
Published by Concordia Publishing House
3558 S. Jefferson Avenue, St. Louis, MO 63118-3968
Manufactured in the United States of America

Library of Congress Cataloging-in-Publication Data
Gorman, Carol.
    Brian's Footsteps/Carol Gorman.
        p.   cm.   —(I witness)
    Summary: Justin has a hard time following in the footsteps of his athletic, smart, handsome brother, until an accident helps Justin and his family understand that each individual is precious in God's eyes.
    ISBN 0-570-04629-7 (lib. bdg.) :
    [1. Family life—Fiction. 2. Brothers—Fiction. 3. Christian life—Fiction.] I. Title. II. Series: Gorman, Carol I witness.
PZ7.G6693Br 1994
[Fic]—dc20
                                                            93-38322

---

1   2   3   4   5   6   7   8   9   10   03   02   01   00   99   98   97   96   95   94

For My Husband, Ed

I Witness

Series

Contents

1

In Training

Keep your head up!" my dad called out from the bleachers at the side of the track.

I raised my head and kept running hard.

I had the whole track to myself. This was my Saturday morning "training session." That's what Dad called it. Every Saturday, Dad and I went to the high school track, and I practiced running.

I was in fifth grade and Dad was coaching me. He wanted me to become a star athlete like my brother Brian.

"If you excel in athletics, you can get a scholarship to a good college the way Brian did," my dad always said. "You can become a coach and make something of yourself."

That was important to my dad, that I "make something" of myself. I'm not the best student around.

Brian *is* a great student. Straight A's all the way through high school. He didn't need an athletic scholarship because he was so smart. But he got one anyway.

Brian is good at everything.

I rounded the last curve in the track and crossed the finish line that my dad had dug in the dirt with his heel.

"Better by a tenth of a second," he called out, as I slowed my pace. "But you can do better. I know you can."

I slowed to a walk and headed back toward the bleachers. Dad was looking at his stopwatch. "Brian was running this time nearly a year ahead of you."

What I *wanted* to say was "Who cares?" but I didn't. I put my hands on my head to draw in all the oxygen I could, and I kept walking.

"You just need to *push* more, Justin," Dad said. "I don't think you're running your best."

I *was* running my best. But I'd never convince Dad of that. If I wasn't running as fast as Wonderful Brian did at my age, Dad thought I wasn't working hard enough.

"Take another minute to cool down," Dad said, "and then we'll go home. Your mom asked me to stop at the grocery store on the way home.

We'll pick up some things for Brian's party tomorrow."

Brian was coming home from college tonight for spring break. Mom and Dad were having a big barbecue in the backyard for him tomorrow night. I think they'd invited practically the whole town.

Dad threw me a towel, and I wiped the sweat from my face and neck.

"You'll do better next time," Dad said. "You're improving slowly. But I wish you'd show what you can do at the track meets."

I wished I did too. I'm never at my best during the metro meets. That's when schools from all over town come together for track events. I get nervous, I guess. Dad is always in the stands and all my friends are there, either running or watching.

"You just have to get tough, mentally," my dad said as we walked to the car. "You let the other boys psych you out. Just don't pay attention to them. Focus on your job, which is running to the finish line."

"Okay," I said. I wished he'd start talking about something else.

We drove to the grocery store and parked. Dad turned off the motor.

"Want me to come in?" I asked.

"No, I have a list here," Dad said. "I'll just be a few minutes."

He got out of the car and walked into the grocery store. I rolled down the window and turned the key in the ignition so I could play the radio. I turned on the music and sat back and closed my eyes.

I love music. I bought myself a secondhand guitar and taught myself how to play some chords. Sometimes I even sing if I'm alone in my room. I don't have a terrific voice. My friend, Paul Bixby, and I get together and play a lot. We also listen to CD's and try to copy some of the chords we hear. It's hard but fun.

The radio was playing a song that was really popular. The chord progressions sounded hard, but I listened to them and tried to play them in my mind. I thought I could play some of them.

"Hi, Justin." The voice came from outside the open car window. I opened my eyes and saw Mandy Jordan, my brother's girlfriend.

"Hi, Mandy," I said, sitting up.

Mandy's a year younger than Brian, so she's in her last year of high school.

She grinned. The breeze was playing with her long, dark hair, and she folded her arms over her chest.

"So Brian's plane comes in at 8:00 tonight?" she asked.

"Yeah," I said. "I think so."

"I bet you're pretty excited to see him again," Mandy said. "I sure am! I haven't seen him since Christmas break."

"Yeah," I said.

I like Mandy, and I sure wasn't going to tell her the truth, that I wasn't excited to see Brian again. In fact, I wished he wasn't coming home. I wished he'd just stay at college and never come home.

"You think you'll go to the airport to meet him?" Mandy asked.

I shrugged. "I don't know. I s'ppose."

"Have him call me the *minute* he gets home," Mandy said. "Okay?"

"Okay."

"Promise?" she said.

"Yeah."

"I got a new outfit that I want to wear the first time I see him," Mandy said. "It cost me a whole week's wages."

Mandy worked at the Dairy Queen down on Morning Glory Boulevard.

"Wow," I said. I didn't know how much a whole week's wages was, but it must have been a lot.

"Well," she said, still smiling, "see you later, Justin."

"See you," I said.

I watched her go. Brian was lucky. He had everything: looks, brains, athletic talent, lots of friends, and a nice girlfriend. What else could anybody want?

"Hello there, Justin," said a low, friendly voice.

I turned and squinted into the sun. His head blocked the sun, so I could hardly see his face. Then he stepped to one side. It was Doc Rybolt. He was getting older, close to retirement. I heard Mom say that not too long ago. He had a little gray hair that was smoothed over the top part of his head, which was bald.

"Hi, Doc," I said.

"So Brian's coming home, eh?" he said. He rested his elbow on the car and leaned in the window.

"Yeah," I said.

Didn't anybody in this town have anything else to talk about?

"It'll be good to see him again," Doc said. "I'm looking forward to the party. Your mom going to fix her famous potato salad?"

"I think so," I said.

Doc ruffled my hair and laughed softly. "Well, I'll be there for sure, then." He looked around him at the sky. "Nice day for Brian to get home." He turned back to me. "You going to be a great athlete like your brother?"

I shrugged. "I don't know," I said.

"Mighty big shoes to fill," Doc said.

"Hmmm?"

"Brian's," Doc said. "It's hard following in Brian's footsteps, I bet."

"Yeah," I said. He didn't know *how* hard.

Just then my dad appeared carrying a sack of groceries.

He smiled when he saw Doc.

"Doc!" Dad said. He shook Doc's hand. "Good to see you! You coming to the party?"

"Wouldn't miss it," Doc said. He nodded at me. "I was just saying to old Justin here that it must be hard to follow Brian, with all of his successes."

"Sure it is," my dad said, "but Justin can be just as successful if he'd put his mind to it."

"I'm sure he can," Doc said and patted my shoulder. "Well, I promised Claudia I'd be right back with a quart of buttermilk. She's making pancakes for brunch. Bad for the waistline, but so good in the mouth." He laughed.

"See you, Doc," I said.

"Bye, Doc," Dad said. "See you tomorrow."

"You bet!" Doc said. "I brought that boy of yours into the world, and I'm very proud of him. I'll be there with bells on."

He waved and sauntered off toward the store.

Dad got in and started the car.

"See that? See how much people respect Brian?" Dad said. "That's because he's worked so hard."

Maybe, I thought. Brian sometimes worked hard, but most of what he did came easily to him. He got good grades without having to study a whole lot. And he was the star of the high school basketball and track teams without having to push himself very hard. He liked sports and was just naturally good at them.

Dad and I rode home in silence. Dad was probably thinking about how great it was going to be to see Brian, and I just stared out the window, wishing colleges didn't have spring breaks.

"Don't go too far," Dad said after we pulled into the garage. "We've got a lot of yard work to do this afternoon to get ready for the party."

"Okay," I said.

We went inside. I took the stairs up to my room two at a time. Mom would be calling us to lunch soon, but I had time to practice a little. I got out my guitar and tried to play the song I'd heard on the radio.

I didn't do it very well. It was really hard. I wished I could take some guitar lessons. But I knew what my dad would say to that: Money is tight now with Brian in college, and we don't have money for extras. Maybe if I earned some more money and bought the CD and listened to it over and over, I could figure out some more of it.

I strummed my guitar and thought about Brian. Brian was like the hero coming home, and I had to be the workhorse getting things ready for him.

I knew I was jealous of Brian. I talked to God about it a lot. But so far He hadn't given me any clear messages telling me how to handle it.

I heard Doc's words coming back to me in my head. *It's hard following in Brian's footsteps, I bet.*

Yeah, it was. And Doc didn't know the half of it.

2

Brian's Party

Justin, honey, will you carry this lemonade out to the serving table?" Mom said. "I think our first guests have arrived."

I could hear voices at the front door.

"There he is!" a big voice boomed out. "The man of honor!"

Then Brian's voice: "Hello, Mr. Henderson. Mrs. Henderson. Good to see you again. I'm glad you could come."

"Hello, Brian," came Mrs. Henderson's voice. "Welcome home."

Then Mr. Henderson's voice: "Wouldn't have missed it for the world, young man!"

I carried the lemonade out the back door and over to the big picnic table on the patio. I set the jug next to the big coffee urn and the paper cups. The table was already filled with covered casseroles and salads, chips and relishes. Mom had gone all out for this party.

There wasn't going to be much to do now till everybody left. Except mingle.

I hate to mingle.

The Hendersons came out the back door with my dad and Brian.

Brian had more muscles and was a little taller than he had been at Christmas. He said he'd been taking weight training in P.E. He was wearing a new yellow polo shirt that Mandy had given him as a welcome-home present; with his wavy blond hair and his perfect, white teeth he looked like a movie star or something.

"What are you majoring in at that school of yours?" Mr. Henderson asked him.

"I'm in premed," Brian said.

"Ah, medicine. A noble profession," Mr. Henderson said, nodding his approval.

"I'm sure you'll make a wonderful doctor," said Mrs. Henderson.

Brian grinned. "I hope so."

I went inside.

"Hel-lo-o!" The heavy front door was standing open, and a large group of people was crowding through the screen door: Aunt Lydia, Uncle Al, and my cousin, Gary; Pastor and Mrs. Lekvoldt; Mandy

Harris with her parents; and Brian's friends, Pete Crawford and Randy Beckman.

Mom's head popped out from the kitchen. "Justin, will you greet these people? I have to take the rolls out of the oven, and your dad is in the backyard with the Hendersons. I'll be there shortly."

"What should I say—?" I said, but Mom had already disappeared back into the kitchen.

I turned back toward the people at the door.

"Well, hello, Justin!" said Uncle Al.

"Hi," I said.

"Where's that brother of yours?" Uncle Al asked.

"Out back," I answered.

"He's in the backyard?" asked Mandy.

"Uh-huh," I said.

Everybody smiled at me as they passed me and headed through the living room. Gary, who is a year younger than I am, went by grinning and socked me on my arm. Like a herd of cattle, one following the other, they all tromped through the living room, into the family room, and out the back door.

I looked at the clock on the mantle. It was 5:05. The party still had two hours and fifty-five minutes to go. I wondered if I'd make it.

I didn't want to get roped into greeting any more people, so I decided to get lost in the crowd outside.

I went out the back door and filled a plate with food. Then I wandered over to the ash tree and leaned against it. It was as good a place as any to eat.

Mandy spotted me and came over holding a cup of lemonade. She didn't have any food. I realized then that I'd never seen Mandy eat.

"Aren't you hungry?" I asked her.

"No, I'm too excited to eat," she said. She looked at my plate heaped with food. "I guess you're not." She laughed. It was a nice laugh.

She scanned the crowd.

"Where did Brian go?" she asked.

"I don't know," I said.

"Oh, there he is," she said. "Doesn't he look great in that shirt?"

"Yeah," I said.

A smile came to her lips, and she followed Brian with her gaze as he walked across the yard with Mr. and Mrs. Maynard.

"We're going to a movie later," she said, still watching him.

"Uh-huh."

"Then maybe out for pizza."

I wondered if Mandy would eat any.

"I have the whole week planned!" she said. "But I wish our schools had spring break at the same time Brian's did. I'm missing out on so much time with him!"

Her eyes were on Brian now as he posed for a picture with Uncle Al and Aunt Lydia. She seemed in a world of her own.

"You should have some of Mom's potato salad," I said. "It's really good."

"Uh-huh," she said.

She wasn't listening. I *knew* she wasn't listening.

"I thought after the party I'd go ice fishing," I said. "In the Arctic."

"Oh, really?" She was still focused on Brian.

"Then I thought I'd rob a couple of banks."

"Oh," she said and nodded.

A few seconds later she must have played back the tape recorder in her head.

"What?" she said, turning toward me. "Did you say you were going to *rob banks?*"

I grinned.

She laughed and gave me a playful shove. "Oh, you!"

The rest of the evening crawled by, with people coming and going.

At seven-thirty, with a half hour to go, some of my brother's friends decided to organize some races in the backyard.

Pete Crawford, who had been on the high school track team with my brother, challenged Brian to a race from the edge of our garage, around the lilac bush, and back. Everybody gathered to watch.

"Brian, you're in your good clothes!" my mother called out to him.

"Yeah, but he's wearing his running shoes," Uncle Al shouted back. "That's what's *really* important!"

Everybody laughed.

Pete and Brian got set at the starting line and Uncle Al shouted, "Get ready. Get set. GO!" The guys took off.

Brian won easily and the crowd applauded and cheered.

Then there were races between some of the other guys. Mandy joined them with some of the girls in Brian's and her classes.

I was watching from the other side of the garage. My dad was standing with Mom at the finish line, looking proud every time Brian won a race, which, of course, was every time he ran.

"Come on, Dennis," Uncle Al called out to my dad. "Let's get up a race with us old-timers."

My dad laughed. Then he and Uncle Al organized a race with six other men. They all looked pretty out-of-shape and full of Mom's food, but they agreed to run anyway.

Brian called out the "Go!" and off they went. It was really funny, watching those guys run. My dad and Uncle Al took the race seriously, while the others laughed all the way around the lilac bush and back.

Dad won, but not by much. The others were right behind him, except for Mr. Farley who had tripped over his own feet and was still sprawled out on the lawn when the others crossed the finish line.

The adults had a good laugh over that.

"Okay, you're next," a voice said next to me. It was Gary.

"Nah," I said. "I've got to go inside and help Mom."

"Go ahead, Justin," Dad said, winking at me. "Race with Gary. You can help your mother later."

"Yeah, let's see you run," said Uncle Al. "See if you got any of that athletic talent that Brian's got."

Just then Brian walked up to us. "You going to run, Sport?" he asked.

I really didn't want to race in front of all these people. "I don't think—" I started to say.

"Sure he is!" said my dad. "Come on, boys. Starting line's here."

"I'll hold your cake," Mandy said. She took it from my hand.

Everybody at the party crowded around the start/finish line to watch. Suddenly, I was nervous. *Very* nervous. Much more nervous than I am at the metro track meets.

"You can beat him," Brian whispered to me. "Gary's a year younger than you."

"That doesn't mean anything," I whispered back.

I whispered a prayer, asking God for help to run my best.

Gary was already standing at the starting line with a big grin on his face. I walked up to him and put my toe on the line.

"Get ready," called out Brian. "Get set. GO!"

And we took off.

The lilac bush was at the far corner of the yard. I ran as fast as I could toward that bush, hearing people shouting our names on both sides of us.

We were neck and neck around the bush, but Gary pulled out ahead of me on the trip back to the garage. I gave it everything I had and closed the gap between us.

But he won. He crossed the line about a second before I did.

People smiled and clapped and congratulated Gary.

My father called out, "Justin, you let your younger cousin *beat* you!"

I glanced over at him. He was shaking his head as if he couldn't believe it. I could tell he was embarrassed that I didn't win.

I walked into the house and up the stairs to my room.

I wasn't hungry anymore.

3

Arguing with Dad

Justin," my father said from behind my bedroom door. I stopped strumming my guitar and listened. "Stop pouting and come out and help your mother clean up."

I strummed my guitar again.

"Did you hear me?" my dad said.

"Yes, I heard you."

"Put that guitar down and come out of your room," he said.

"It was Brian's party," I said, still strumming. I knew I shouldn't talk like that to my dad, and I knew I was heading for trouble, but I was mad enough that I didn't care. "I got the yard ready for the party, so he should do the cleanup."

"Don't talk back to me!" my dad said. "Put that guitar down and open this door!"

I set my guitar on my bed. I went to the door and opened it. "I'm not pouting," I said quietly.

"Sure you are," Dad said, pushing his way inside. "You're mad at yourself because a kid younger than you won that race."

"I didn't want to run," I said. "I *said* I didn't want to race him."

"And back away from a challenge?" my dad said.

"Why did I have to race him?" I said.

"You could have beaten him," Dad said. "You *should* have beaten him."

I didn't say anything.

"You should at least have been mature about it," my dad said. "Shake his hand. Smile and say congratulations. But don't tuck your tail between your legs and run to your room like a beaten puppy!"

"I didn't do that!" I said.

"You sure did," Dad said.

Well, maybe I had sort of run up to my room because I was embarrassed. But it wasn't because I'd lost the race. It was just that my dad had made such a big deal out of my losing.

I hated letting my dad down. But we can't all be perfect like Brian.

I looked at the floor and stayed cool. "You yelled out, 'Justin, you let your younger cousin *beat* you.'"

"Well, you *did* let your younger cousin beat you!" my dad said. He sighed with a kind of frustrated sound. "Justin, you're going to have to develop a tougher hide," he said.

"What do you mean?" I asked.

"You have to learn to accept criticism," he said. "Brian doesn't act like this."

"Brian never loses," I said.

"That's the most ridiculous thing you've ever said!"

Dad's face was turning red, so I knew he was really getting mad. "And I've heard enough of your whining. Get downstairs and help your mother clean up. Now!"

I knew better than to argue with him when he was really mad. It would only get worse if I said anything else.

So I went downstairs to help Mom.

"Here, listen to this," I said. "I figured this out yesterday."

On Monday afternoon after school, I sat on the edge of Paul Bixby's bed and played my guitar.

Paul sat on the floor with his instrument and listened to me play the song I'd heard on the radio. He nodded as I played and started to smile.

"Cool," he said, when I'd finished. "What was that weird chord progression in the bridge?"

I showed him, and he tried it on his guitar. "Man, that's hard," he said. "I could never've figured that out."

This is why I like Paul. He gets as excited about music as I do. And when I play something really well, he tells me.

I guess I'm a sucker for compliments.

Mrs. Bixby poked her head in the door. "Sounds great, guys," she said.

"Thanks," Paul said. "Justin's teaching me some good stuff."

"Well," she said, smiling, "keep it up, Justin. Why don't you stay for dinner tonight and you can both play for Paul's dad?"

I'd been waiting for an invitation like that for months. Mr. Bixby loves music. In fact, he plays the piano sometimes on the weekends at a little club downtown. Paul's dad is some kind of businessman, but at heart he's a jazz musician. I had always hoped that some day Paul and I could jam with him in the living room around the piano. I mean, Paul and I were beginners and not very good compared with a real musician, but it would be so much fun—

And tonight I got an invitation to play for him.

But I couldn't stay tonight. It was because of Brian, of course. I was supposed to be thrilled that he was home. I was supposed to spend every minute I could with him.

And that meant dinner with the family.

"Sorry, Mrs. Bixby," I said. "I sure wish I could—"

"That's all right, Justin," she said. "Maybe some other time."

"Great."

Why did Brian have to come home from college?

And that was when the thought first came to me. *I wish Brian weren't my brother. I wish he'd never been born.*

It was a horrible thing to think, and it shocked me. But I got used to having the thought in my mind, and over the next several days, it became more comfortable, like a broken-in shoe. I turned to it every time I was mad about Wonderful Brian.

I knew it was wrong to think about my brother that way, and I figured God probably was pretty ticked off with me. But I couldn't help it. That's how I felt.

At dinner that evening Mom fixed Brian's favorite dish—pot roast.

"Mandy and I hiked five miles of the Peppercorn Trail after she got out of school this afternoon," Brian said at dinner.

Mom handed him a bowl of mashed potatoes. "Have some more potatoes, honey," she said. "You don't have to worry about calories."

"Thanks, but this is enough," Brian said.

Mom looked at me. "Justin, would you like them?"

"Yeah, thanks," I said.

I looked up just in time to see Mom give Dad a "meaningful" look. She nodded at me.

"So," my dad said, pausing to clear his voice. "What did *you* do today, Justin?"

Mom must have told him to talk to me the way he talks to Brian.

I didn't answer his question for a second. Dad isn't exactly a fan of my guitar playing.

"I went over to Paul's," I said.

"Paul Bixby?" Brian asked.

"Yeah."

"He seems like a nice guy," Brian said.

"Yeah, he is."

"Is he on your track team?" Dad asked.

"No," I said. Here it comes, I thought.

31

"Well, what did you and this Paul do all afternoon?" Dad asked.

"We played our guitars," I said.

Dad frowned right on cue. "I see."

"What else does Paul do?" Dad asked.

"What do you mean?" I said.

"I mean, is he a good student?" he said. "Or an athlete?"

"He gets okay grades, I think," I said. "He doesn't play any sports at school."

Dad frowned again. "That's it?"

I was starting to get mad. "Yeah, Dad," I said. "That's it."

"Honey—" Mom said. She gave Dad another "meaningful" look.

Dad ignored her. "So what does Paul want to do when he grows up?"

"I don't know, Dad," I said. I was getting madder by the minute.

"Paul has lots of time to decide," my mother said smoothly. "He's only in fifth grade."

"He could teach music if he wanted to," Brian suggested.

"Not if his grades aren't good enough to get into college," Dad said. "Justin, you're going to have to put your nose to the grindstone if you want

32

to go to college. Either that or work hard for a track scholarship."

"I thought we were talking about Paul," I said.

"Let's have a pleasant dinner," Mom said.

"I'm talking about you," Dad said, his voice getting louder. "We never had to have these arguments with Brian!"

"Dad—" Brian started to say.

"Just *stop!*" I yelled. "Everybody stop! I'm sick of getting compared to Wonderful Brian all the time." I shoved my chair back to stand up, and it fell backward on the floor. "I'm not Brian, in case you haven't noticed. I'm *me!* So just leave me alone!"

I threw my napkin down on my plate, stomped out of the room, and out the front door.

4

Greg Madison

I grabbed my bike in the garage and headed off down the street. I didn't know where I was going. I didn't care.

After fifteen minutes of riding I found myself in the park. I stopped at a green bench under a maple that was just beginning to sprout leaves.

I leaned my bike against the tree and sat down on the bench. My heart was still racing, and I was still mad.

Why did Dad have to give me such a hard time? He was always on my case about something.

I looked up into the tree branches that swayed a little in the spring night air. It was good to be alone for awhile, away from my house.

I thought about Dad and his training sessions and his advice and all the comparisons between Brian and me.

I knew I shouldn't have yelled at my dad. I never used to yell at him. But the last several months I'd started losing my temper sometimes.

Boy, that really makes him mad.

I don't like the way it feels when I get mad and yell. I love my dad. But sometimes I get angry at myself because I can't be what he wants me to be.

And I end up yelling at him.

I remembered that Mrs. Jenkins, my Sunday school teacher, read us something from the Bible once that said we're supposed to "honor" our father and mother. I suppose that means we shouldn't lip off and say angry things even though we *feel* angry sometimes.

I wished I didn't feel mad at my dad. I don't like to fight with anyone. I've asked God to forgive me a million times. I've even asked Him to help Dad like me for what I am.

I just wished he'd let me be *me*. I didn't want to be Brian's brother. I wanted to be Justin Talbot, myself.

"Hi." The voice startled me. It came from the other side of the maple.

I turned around, and he stepped out from behind the tree.

He was thin and kind of tall with dark hair, and he looked a little older than me.

"Hi," I said.

"Nice bike," he said. He leaned over and examined the drive train, brakes, and rims.

"Thanks," I said.

"Mind if I take a ride on it?" he asked. He was still bent over, looking at it.

His question really surprised me. I didn't know what to say. I mean, it was an expensive bike, and I'd worked for over a year to earn half of the money for it. My dad had paid for the other half.

And I didn't even know this guy.

He looked up at me. "Mind if I take it for a ride?" he said again.

I shrugged and kind of smiled. I didn't want him to think I was a jerk or something.

"I don't even know you," I said.

He laughed. "You can trust me, man. I'll bring your bike back. I just want to ride it for a minute."

"A minute?" I said.

"Yeah," he said. He looked back over his shoulder. "See the wading pool down there by the big tree?"

There was a sidewalk along the edge of the park. It went down and turned at the big oak next to the wading pool, then continued on out of sight, down the slope to the big fenced-in swimming pool.

"Yeah," I said.

"I'll ride it down the sidewalk. When I get as far as that tree, I'll come back."

I looked at him closer. He looked okay, but I really didn't want him to ride my bike.

I thought hard. I didn't know how to get out of this. What should I do?

I didn't know.

"Well, okay," I said.

He grinned and grabbed my bike. He ran a few steps, threw his leg over the side, and took off down the sidewalk.

I watched him with my heart beating hard. I could hear myself trying to explain to my family what had happened. *I let this kid ride my bike, and he rode off with it and didn't come back.*

"Why did you let him ride your bike?" my mom would ask.

"Because he asked if he could," I'd say. "He said he'd bring it right back."

"And you didn't even know the boy?" my father would say. "What could you've been thinking!"

I stood there, watching the guy riding away on my bike, and I felt really stupid. Why did I let him take it?

What should I have said when he asked if he could ride it?

It all happened so fast, I couldn't think of what to do.

I felt like an idiot. I should have told him no. I should have said I had to get home, that I didn't have time for him to ride it.

He was almost at the turn in the sidewalk. That was when he was supposed to come back. He'd said he would.

He was going pretty fast. He didn't look as if he'd be able to turn around, going that fast.

Justin, you idiot! I said to myself.

The guy reached the turn in the sidewalk. And he kept going, down over the slope, and he disappeared.

My heart stopped. He'd stolen my bike!

I started running toward the tree. Where had he gone? Would I ever find him again and get my bike back?

Then I saw him. Just his head, at first, as he came back up over the slope. Then the rest of him.

He was heading back toward me.

I stopped running and watched him.

I could see him grinning. He was having a good time on my bike. He whooped as he came near.

"Great bike, man!" he said. He rode it around the tree. "Great bike."

"Thanks," I said. My heart was beating double time.

"Wish I had one like it."

"Thanks," I said. "I like it too."

"Hey, what's your name?" he asked me.

"Justin Talbot," I said.

He kept riding around the tree.

"What's your name?" I asked him.

"Greg Madison," he said. "Where you go to school?"

"Wilkin," I said. "What school do you go to?"

He stopped the bike and walked it to the tree. He leaned it against the trunk.

"Cleveland," he said.

Cleveland Junior High was about a half mile away.

"You waiting for someone?" Greg asked.

"No," I said.

"I am," he said. "For a friend. We're going over to his house to listen to CD's."

I nodded.

"You got some good CD's?" he asked.

"Yeah, some," I said. I told him what I had.

"You got some good stuff," he said. "You want to come and bring your CD's?"

Another invitation. Boy, was I popular today. It made me feel kind of good that Greg—who was at least two years older than me—wanted me to come with him.

But, of course, I couldn't. I'd had to leave my house to blow off steam. But I needed to get back. If I stayed out very long, my dad would be even madder.

"I can't," I said. "I have to get home."

"Maybe some other time," he said.

"Sure," I said. "That'd be great. See you."

I got on my bike and headed back home.

Mom and Dad didn't say anything to me about the argument when I got back. That was because they weren't home. They'd gone over to a neighbor's house for some reason.

Brian was in his room polishing a pair of dress shoes. I'd never seen him do that before.

"Hi, Sport," he said when he saw me.

"Hi," I said. I leaned against the door frame. "Why are you doing that?"

"Polishing my shoes? Because Mandy and I are going to a symphony concert in a half hour."

"Really?" I said. "I didn't know you liked music that much."

He shrugged. "I have to get cultured sometime," he said.

"Where'd you get the tickets?" I asked him.

"Uncle Al and Aunt Lydia couldn't use their tickets tonight," Brian said. "So they gave them to me."

A familiar feeling stirred in me.

"Why didn't they give the tickets to me?" I asked.

"What do you mean?"

"I mean, I'm the music person in this family," I said. "Why wouldn't they give *me* the tickets?"

Brian shrugged. "I guess because I'm home for vacation. They thought they'd be nice—"

"Why do you always get everything!" I said angrily. I didn't like the way I sounded. I knew Dad would say I was whining, but I didn't care. "Why does everybody think you're so great, anyway?"

"Pipe down!" Brian said angrily. "What's the matter with you, Justin? Ever since I got home, you've been mad or moping around!"

"Leave me alone," I said and stomped down the hall toward my room.

41

"Grow up, Justin!" Brian yelled after me. "Sometimes other people are going to get a pat on the back or a surprise gift. Sometimes they deserve it!"

I slammed my door behind me and fell onto my bed.

I hate Brian! I thought. Why can't he just go back to school and never come home again?

It felt as if a worm of anger that had crawled into my stomach about a year ago had grown into a gigantic, ugly snake that was now rolling around in my belly, squeezing everything else out of the way.

Brian gets everything! I thought.

If you had made me take truth serum right then, I'd probably have to say that I didn't care all that much about the symphony. Classical music is not my favorite kind.

But that was beside the point.

Uncle Al and Aunt Lydia had decided to give the tickets to Brian and not me.

Wonderful Brian wins again.

It took several minutes for me to calm down. I stretched out on the bed on my stomach, and I thought again about my Sunday school teacher, Mrs. Jenkins.

She told us that Jesus loves everybody. She said His example helps us love everyone, even our enemies.

But how can we be expected to love our enemies if we can't even like our own brother?

I wasn't like Brian. And since everyone wanted me to be like him, they were disappointed.

Even me.

But I can't be somebody I'm not, I thought. *And I won't even try.*

5

An Afternoon with Greg

Justin," my mom said. "It's for you."

It was Wednesday after school. I was sitting at the kitchen table having a snack. Brian had gone to pick up Mandy at school.

Mom stood next to the phone on the kitchen desk. I got up from the table, leaving my cereal to soak in the bowl.

"Hello?" I said.

"Hey, Justin?" the voice said.

"Yeah?"

"You want to come over and bring your CD's?"

I didn't recognize the voice.

"Who's this?" I asked.

"Greg," he said. "I saw you yesterday in the park."

"Oh, yeah," I said.

"You want to bring your CD's and come over?" he repeated.

"Sure!" I said. I'd never had a big kid call me before. "Where do you live?"

"On Ash Street, 1702."

It was about a mile and a half from my house.

"When?" I asked.

"Now," he said. "Don't forget your CD's."

"Okay," I said.

"Oh, and Justin?" he said.

"Yeah?"

"Can you get some cigs?"

"Some what?"

"Cigarettes. Your parents smoke?"

"My dad does," I said.

"Can you bring some with you?" he asked.

"Uh—no," I said. "They aren't mine."

"Just bring two," he said. "One for me and one for my friend. See you soon."

He hung up.

I stood there with the receiver in my hand. Mom turned from the kitchen sink.

"Who was that, honey?" she asked.

"A guy," I said. I hung up.

She smiled. "I know that," she said. "What is the guy's name?"

"Greg Madison," I said. "I'm going over to his house to listen to CD's."

"Oh, that's nice," she said. She frowned. "I don't think I've heard his name before. Greg Madison. Is he in your class at school?"

"No," I said. I didn't want her to ask me what class he was in. She might not want me to hang around with an older guy, so I kept talking. "Well, I've got to go. I told him I'd be right over."

"Hold on," Mom said. "Write down his address so I know where you are."

"Okay." I wrote it down.

"Aren't you going to finish your snack?" she asked.

"No," I said. "I ate as much as I wanted."

I carried the cereal bowl and juice glass to the sink.

"Okay," she said. "But remember, you promised your dad you'd go over to the track to train this afternoon. You've got a metro meet in a couple of days."

I rolled my eyes. "Yeah, okay," I said. "I'll go over to the high school track before I come home from Greg's."

Mom nodded. "Dinner's at six."

I scooted out of the kitchen.

I went up to my room and picked out six CD's that I liked and thought Greg would like. I put them into my backpack.

I smiled to myself as I hurried down the stairs. I couldn't believe that a big kid wanted to be with me. It made me feel great. Maybe my life was getting better.

Greg had said to bring two cigarettes. I knew Dad kept his cigarettes in his desk in the den.

I went downstairs, into the den and opened the top left drawer of the desk. There it was. A package of cigarettes.

Dad knew he shouldn't smoke. He'd tried to stop a couple of times, but couldn't. He'd cut way down on them, though. Now he only allows himself three cigarettes a day—one after each meal.

It would be so easy to take two cigarettes, I thought. He'd never miss them, and the guys would be glad they'd invited me over.

But that was stealing, taking something that didn't belong to me.

It was wrong, and I couldn't do it.

I closed the desk drawer and walked out of the den and out the front door. I'd make up an excuse to Greg why I didn't have them.

I rode my bike over to the address Greg had given me and knocked on the door. There was loud music playing inside. I could hear it coming from a window at the side of the upstairs.

I knocked hard on the door and waited.

Nobody came.

I knocked louder this time.

Still nobody came.

I wondered if I should go home. I didn't think Greg would ever hear me with the music so loud inside.

Then the front door was yanked open, and Greg stood there.

"Come on in," he said, opening the screen door. "What CD's did you bring?"

I opened my backpack and showed him.

"Cool," he said. "Come on. We're upstairs."

I followed Greg up the wooden staircase and into his room at the top of the stairs.

The shades were pulled, and except for the narrow bands of daylight that peeked in from the edges of the two windows, his room was in shadows.

A heavy cloud of cigarette smoke clung to the air. The place really stunk.

I suddenly felt really uncomfortable. This guy was different from me. Different from Brian, too, and all the other guys I knew.

Through the dark haze, I saw a kid with shoulder-length blond hair sprawled out on the bed. His elbow rested on the bed, propping up his head which rested on his hand.

"This is Dan Schneider," Greg said, pointing to the guy.

"Hi," I said to him.

"Hi," he said. He looked sleepy or bored, I couldn't tell which. "D'you bring the cigs?"

"No," I said.

Dan groaned and fell backward onto the pillow.

"You didn't bring 'em?" Greg said, stepping forward, a frown on his face.

"No," I said. "I looked in my Dad's drawer, but they were gone."

So I lied. I don't usually do that, but then I'd rather do that than steal from my parents. Besides, I didn't want to look like a baby in front of these older guys and say I didn't want to take the cigarettes. They'd think I was scared to do it.

I wasn't scared. I just didn't *want* to steal the cigarettes.

I turned to Greg. "Isn't your mom home?" I asked. I couldn't believe they'd be smoking if she was.

"No," he said and laughed as if he'd read my mind. "I do what I want whether she's here or not."

I've heard kids my age say stuff like that, and I didn't really believe them. When Greg said it, though, I had the feeling he was telling the truth.

He grabbed the top CD from the pile I was holding, slipped it out of its case and put it into the CD player.

He poked the PLAY button.

Dan recognized the album right away.

"Cool," he said, not moving from the bed.

And that's how we spent the next hour: sitting in Greg's dark, smoky bedroom, listening to my CD's.

Greg and Dan mostly talked to themselves. They played parts of all the CD's I'd brought. Dan complained a couple of times that he didn't have any cigarettes to smoke.

It didn't take me long to start feeling ticked off. I mean, these guys were using me.

I don't like being used.

They'd invited me over just so I would bring my CD's and my dad's cigarettes. Then they ignored me and complained that I hadn't stolen the "cigs" from Dad.

I sat there on the floor of Greg's room and watched those guys and decided it wasn't such an honor getting invited to Greg's house. If I didn't have CD's, I wouldn't have been invited.

"I have to leave now," I said after the music had stopped the next time.

"But we haven't heard the other side of this CD," Greg said.

"Yeah, I know," I said, "but I have to go."

"Go where?" Dan said.

"To train. I run at the high school track."

Dan snorted and rolled over on the bed to face the wall. "He *trains* at the track."

Greg shrugged. "So just leave the CD here," he said. "I'll get it back to you tomorrow."

"No," I said. I was through being used. "I gotta go."

I gathered up the CD's and walked out of the room.

"What's with him?" I heard Dan say as I headed down the stairs.

Greg didn't even follow me to the front door, but I heard them laughing behind me.

I pulled open the front door, crossed the porch, and walked down to the front sidewalk.

I couldn't wait to get away from there. The guys, their smoky room, the whole place gave me the creeps.

I thought about Paul. I couldn't wait to get together with him again.

Training with my dad didn't even sound so bad right now.

6

The Stolen CD

It's funny how a couple of jerks can make you appreciate your own family and friends. After spending an hour with Greg and Dan, I was ready to go back to my normal life.

Even training with Dad.

The next Metro track meet was coming up on Saturday afternoon, so I trained hard for the next couple of days after school.

I even invited my dad to come and work with me on Thursday after supper. He seemed surprised that I'd asked him, but it didn't stop him from running me hard.

"Get your knees up!" he yelled. "Stay on your toes! Relax your face!"

I ran around and around and around the track.

On the way home from our Thursday night training session, my dad said, "You've worked hard the last several days. And your times were a little better today."

"Yeah," I said. "Thanks."

"See what a little hard work can do?" he said.

"Yeah," I said. It had felt like a *lot* of hard work to me, I thought. But I didn't say it to Dad.

"You're going better," Dad said. "But you still have a ways to go."

"I know."

"Okay now, the meet is just a couple of days away," he said. "I want you to start thinking about it. Don't think about the crowds, or who will be there, but think about that finish line. See it in your mind. You have to get there fast. Faster than any of the other boys."

"Sometimes," I said, "I think of a song in my mind and run in rhythm to the song."

My dad turned to look at me a second. Then he turned back to the road. "Maybe that's your problem," he said.

"What do you mean?"

"You're thinking about music and not about winning," Dad said.

I stiffened in my seat and Dad looked over at me again.

"An athlete has to train his mind as well as his body, Justin," Dad said.

"I'm trying to do that," I said.

"Trying isn't good enough," Dad said. "*Do* it. Focus your concentration. You don't run well at the meets because you can't focus sharply on the job you need to do. You do all right when we practice because there's nothing to distract you."

"Okay," I said.

"Trust me," Dad said. "I know what I'm talking about."

"Okay," I said again.

Agreeing with him was easier than arguing.

It wasn't until Friday after school that I emptied the backpack I'd taken to Greg's with the CD's and realized that they weren't all there.

One CD was missing. It was my favorite. It was also Greg and Dan's favorite.

I thought a minute. I knew I hadn't left the CD at Greg's by mistake. Greg must have swiped the disk and hidden it sometime after we'd listened to it.

I remembered them laughing as I left. Now I knew why.

I bet they thought they were pretty smart, stealing from a younger kid.

My heart started beating hard and my whole body heated up as if I had a fever. Boy, was I mad!

I checked through my stuff one more time to make sure the CD wasn't there. It wasn't.

Then I called to Mom that I'd be right back.

I got on my bike and rode straight back to Greg's house. I didn't expect Dan to be there, but I was hoping Greg would be home.

I found both of them sitting on the front porch step when I arrived. They didn't get up. They looked as lazy and bored as they had the other day.

I stopped my bike right in front of them.

Dan sneered. "Not *training* today?"

"No," I said.

Dan turned to Greg. "He's not training today," he said. His voice was filled with sarcasm.

Greg stared at me, but didn't say anything.

"I came back to get my CD," I told them.

"What CD?" Greg said.

Dan smiled a little and folded his arms over his knees.

"My CD," I said. "The one—" I almost said, *The one you took from me.* But instead, I said, "The one I left here."

"You think I took it?" Greg said.

"No," I said. "I left it here by accident."

"Well, you didn't leave it," Greg said. "I would've seen it after you left."

I got off my bike, leaned it against the porch and started up the porch stairs.

Suddenly, Greg and Dan didn't look lazy anymore. They both jumped to their feet and blocked the top of the stairs.

"Where do you think you're going?" Greg said.

"I want to go upstairs and look for my CD," I said.

"I told you," Greg said. "It's not there."

"I bet it is," I said. "I want to go and look."

"Get off my porch," Greg said.

"Why?" I said.

"Because it's my porch, and I told you to get off."

"My CD's up there," I said.

"I told you it wasn't," Greg said.

"I'm sure it is," I said.

"You calling my friend a liar?" Dan said. He took a step down toward me. "Hmmm?"

"No," I said. I held my ground. "I never called anybody a liar. I just want to go up and look for my CD."

"Get lost, squirt," Greg said. "Get out of my sight."

I took another step toward Dan. "Just let me go up and look once. If I don't find it, I'll leave."

Dan took two steps down fast and shoved me hard. I grabbed for the rail, but missed and fell backward with my arms windmilling in the air.

I fell hard on the ground and cracked my elbow on the cement walk at the bottom of the steps.

"Get lost!" Greg yelled from the porch.

My elbow throbbed with pain.

"Don't ever come around here again!" Dan growled.

I got up, rubbing my elbow. I took my bike, got on, and rode away from Greg's house with the two guys yelling at my back.

I was so stupid! I thought. I tried blinking fast to keep the tears from coming. But they came anyway, fast and hard. They rolled down my face and dropped on my shirt and my arms.

I sniffed and wiped my nose with my wrist.

Those dumb jerks, I thought. Using me was bad enough. But then they pretended to like me so they could steal from me. How could I have been so dumb?

I remembered then what Mrs. Jenkins had said about forgiveness. Jesus forgave even the people who nailed Him to the cross. He's our example for forgiving others.

But I didn't think I could ever forgive Dan and Greg for using me and stealing from me—and asking me to steal from my own father.

That was just too much.

The Metro Track Meet

Saturday afternoon was the Metro track meet. My dad, Mom, Brian, and Mandy were all coming to watch.

That made me nervous. Very nervous. I knew they were hoping for big things from me. They'd be watching every step I took during my races. Dad would probably take a few notes to pass along to me later. You know, do more of this, do less of that.

I hadn't told anybody about what had happened with Greg and Dan. I figured Dad and Brian would tell me how stupid I was to go over there when I didn't even know those guys.

I already knew that myself.

I'd been thinking about how I should forgive them, but I didn't know if I could ever do that. I mean, Jesus was really good at forgiving everyone, but I'm just an average kid. A kid who was still pretty mad about getting his favorite—not to mention, most expensive—CD stolen from him.

The meet on Saturday was held at the high school track, and as soon as we pulled into the parking lot, we could see that the place was crowded with people. They were all wearing colorful sweats or shorts and talking and laughing. I suppose a lot of them were out just to enjoy the bright spring day.

"Looks like a lot of competition," Mandy said. She was squeezed in between Brian and me in the back seat.

"Let's hope Justin can handle it," Brian said. He grinned at me, and I made a face at him. I was too nervous to take any teasing that day.

"A lot of these kids are just out to have fun," Dad said. "They're not serious runners."

Just to have fun. That sounded good. I wished I could run just to have fun. No critiques, no suggestions from anybody. I'd enjoy it a whole lot more.

At the metro meets, any kid in the fourth, fifth, or sixth grade can come and run in the races. A lot of kids from my class showed up to run that day.

"Hey, Justin!" It was Juliet Hollingsworth. She and her friend Tiffany Gallagher were walking toward the track with her mom and two little sisters.

"Hi," I called back.

"Good luck on your races!" she said and gave me the "thumbs up" sign.

"Thanks," I said. "You too."

Juliet's two sisters gave me the "thumbs up" sign too, even though they didn't know me. I heard one of them say, "Who was that?" after they had passed.

Dad, Mom, Mandy, and Brian told me good luck. Dad pulled me aside for some last-minute advice.

"Just remember, Justin, *concentrate*. Don't pay attention to what the other boys or the spectators are doing," he said.

Then they all went to sit in the stands. I watched them go while butterflies flopped around in my stomach.

The first event was the 100-meter dash. Fourth-grade girls were up first. There were so many kids competing that they had to run eight at a time in three different heats. I watched the first few races, then got kind of bored.

I looked up into the stands and saw Paul sitting with some kids from our class. It felt good to see him. Paul was a good friend, and while he cheered for me to win, it wasn't any big deal if I lost.

I started running lightly in place to warm up. After awhile, I stretched out my body to get limber. Most of the other kids were just standing and talking and horsing around. As my dad had said, they didn't take these meets too seriously.

After about twenty minutes, it was time for fifth-grade boys to run the 100 meter dash. I was in the second heat.

When it was my turn, I stood and looked down the starting line at my competition. One of the guys, Ross Hunter, was in my class. He was pretty fast, but I knew I could beat him. I didn't know the other four guys. They were from other schools. The official, dressed all in white, raised his pistol.

"All right, guys," he said in his loud official voice. "Get ready, get set—"

Please help me do my best, Lord, I prayed.

BANG! He fired the blank, and we took off.

I knew my dad was timing me in the stands, and I ran my fastest. I pulled out ahead and kept a narrow lead all the way. It was a close race, but I *won!*

The woman who was timing my lane said congratulations and gave me my time. It wasn't bad, just a hundredth of a second slower than I'd run in the training session with my dad a few days ago.

I looked up to see Dad, Mom, Brian, Mandy, and Paul on their feet, cheering. Then Dad raised his stop watch to look at my time. I couldn't tell from where I was standing what his face was doing.

Kids were clapping me on the back and shaking my hand. I had won the race! That was the first time I'd ever won at a Metro track meet.

Dad *had* to have been happy about that!

I walked around waiting for my breathing to calm down. "Great race, Justin!" some kids from my class yelled to me. I felt great!

I had three more races that afternoon: the 400 meter dash, the 800 meter run, and a relay some of the kids had organized at school this week.

Here's how I did: in the 400 meter dash, I came in second and improved my best time by a tenth of a second. In the 800 meter run, I came in third and slowed my time by two tenths of a second. And our relay team that was led off by Ross Hunter and anchored by me won first place.

It was a good meet. I whispered, "Thank You, God," for His help. I know I couldn't have done that well without Him.

I *had* done my best. I hadn't been as great as Brian was at this age, but it was as good as *I* could do. I hoped my family would be happy.

Paul met me at the side of the stands.

"Great job, Justin!" he said. He slapped my hands and grinned from ear to ear.

"Thanks," I said.

Kids went by from my class and congratulated me on my two wins and two places.

I saw my family coming and said, "Wait, Paul. I want my dad to meet you." I hoped that if Dad met Paul and saw what a nice guy he was, he wouldn't mind my guitar playing so much.

Mom, Dad, Brian, and Mandy walked over.

"Good job, Justin!" Mandy said, beaming.

"I knew you had it in you, Sport," Brian said.

My mom glanced quickly at Dad and then gave me a hug. "I'm proud of you, honey," she said.

"Thanks, Mom," I said and hugged her back.

Dad was quiet.

"Uh, Dad," I said, "I think you're the only person in the family who hasn't met Paul Bixby."

Paul stepped forward and put out his hand.

"Glad to meet you, Mr. Talbot," he said.

My dad shook his hand. "Paul," he said and nodded.

Paul said hi to Mom, Brian, and Mandy.

"Justin was good out there," Paul said to Dad. He looked at me. "You're really getting good!" He slapped me on the back.

"Thanks," I said to Paul.

"He's improving," Dad said.

"Well, I'd better get going," Paul said. "I promised my Dad I'd help him with some yard work today."

"Nice to see you again, Paul," my mom said.

"See you," Brian said.

Dad looked as if he was thinking about something. He nodded and smiled a little at Paul.

Paul left.

He's improving, my dad had said. That was all. I'd *won* two races, and all he said was that I was improving. And he hadn't said anything yet to *me*.

I could feel the blood in my body start to percolate. Dad still wasn't happy with my running.

I'd trained and trained, and I ran as hard as I could this afternoon. But it still wasn't good enough.

What did he want from me?

The Accident

We all got into the car: Dad, Mom, Brian, Mandy, and me. Dad started the car and headed for home. Brian and Mandy kept up a conversation all the way, but I hardly heard any of it.

I sat with them in the back, right behind the driver's seat. I stared at the back of my dad's head. I wished I could look right through his skull and into his mind.

What was he thinking? Was he so quiet because I had let him down? On today of all days? The day I had won, or helped win, two out of four events?

My mom looked back at me, then at my dad, then back again at me.

"What are your plans for the rest of the day, Justin?" she said. Her voice was cheerful. She was trying *too* hard to be cheerful, I thought.

"I don't know," I said.

Actually, I was hoping to go over to Paul's house to listen to music and play our guitars. Paul had a copy of the CD that Greg had swiped from me, and I wanted to listen to it again.

"Can we drop Mandy off at her house?" Brian said. "She's going to change clothes, and then we're going out for dinner."

Dad nodded and turned right at the next corner. We drove three more blocks, then pulled up in front of her two-story brick house.

"See you later, Bri," she said. "And congratulations on a terrific meet, Justin."

"Thanks," I said, and glanced again at the back of my dad's head.

"Thanks for the ride," she said to my dad. "Bye, everybody."

She closed the car door and ran up the front walk toward her house. Dad pulled away from the curb.

That's when he started talking.

"Justin, I realize that you did win a couple of races today," he said. "And I congratulate you for that."

"Thanks," I said. I knew there was more coming. I looked at my mom's face, and she looked kind of anxious.

"But your times weren't very strong," Dad said.

"They weren't bad," I said quietly.

"But you only improved in one race," Dad said. He continued driving toward our house. "That was a tenth of a second, which isn't bad. But in the other races, you were *slower* than usual."

"Justin's been working hard, Dennis," my mom reminded him. "He's been training at the track several times a week, and this is the best meet he's ever had. Let's let him enjoy it."

"He can enjoy it," Dad said. "I'm only saying that he should be working harder. Brian was out there working whenever he got the chance, to improve his times."

"Dad, I *liked* running," Brian said. "If I hadn't enjoyed it so much, I probably wouldn't have—"

"Justin would like running if he really got fast," Dad said. "If his times really improved. Everybody likes what they're good at."

"I won two races, Dad," I said. I could feel the tears threatening to come, and I swallowed hard and cleared my throat.

"You didn't have much competition, Justin," Dad said. "Most of those kids were there because they couldn't think of anything else to do today."

We came to our house, and Dad pulled into the driveway.

"Let's all go out for dinner," my mom said, turning in her seat. She smiled. She was using her let's-smooth-everything-out-and-be-happy voice. "We'll talk about other things and have a nice, leisurely dinner."

"I'm not hungry," I said.

"Now don't start pouting again," Dad said.

"I'm *not* pouting," I said.

"Mandy and I are going out," Brian said. He sounded impatient with all the arguing.

He opened the car door and got out.

"Well," Mom said, "then I'll fix a nice supper at home. Why don't we barbecue, just the three of us? Dennis, what do you think? How about a big, juicy hamburger?"

"I don't care, Helen," Dad said.

Mom's face fell. "Let's try and have a pleasant evening," she said. "Let's not argue. Brian's home, and he'll go back soon. We should try and keep life pleasant—" She didn't finish the sentence.

Keep life pleasant so poor Brian doesn't have to get upset, I thought.

Mom got out of the car. She ducked her head back into the car. "Come on, you two," she said. "Come on inside."

"We'll be in," Dad said. "I want to talk to Justin for a few minutes."

Mom sighed and went around to the back of the house.

Dad turned in his seat. "Come up to the front seat, Justin."

I got out of the car, walked around to the passenger side, and climbed in the front seat. I closed the door next to me. "Justin, you know I love you," Dad said.

I didn't say anything.

"And I want to be proud of you," he said.

My throat suddenly felt very tight. I had thought Dad *was* proud of me—at least a little. I knew he wanted me to be a better runner, and he wanted me to be more like Brian. But I still had thought he was sort of proud of me as a son. I mean, I'm not like Greg Madison. I don't do bad stuff. I don't steal or smoke or drink or use people. I'm polite. I try to be a decent guy.

And I try to be what my dad wants me to be.

I folded my arms across my chest and waited for the rest of his speech.

"Justin," Dad said, "I realize that you are just in fifth grade and that you should have time for fun and even goofing around. For instance, I think you should spend time playing that guitar of yours. You worked hard to earn the money for it. You should have a good time playing it."

"I do," I said.

"But there's a time for hard work too," Dad said. "Even if your heart isn't in it. If that hard work can pay off with great rewards, you should do it even if you don't like it. Everybody doesn't love what they do, Justin, but they do it in order to earn money or build a good life for themselves or their families."

"Maybe if I had music lessons," I said, "I could get a music scholarship—"

"But what can you do with music?" Dad said.

"Just like Brian said," I pointed out, "I could teach."

"But you need good grades to get scholarships," Dad said. "Colleges expect their music students on scholarships to get good grades."

I didn't speak.

"You're not an impressive student, Justin," Dad said.

"I *know* that," I said. I couldn't keep the anger that I was feeling out of my voice. I figured that God might be upset that I wasn't honoring my father right now, but I was too angry to care.

"So you should aim for an athletic scholarship," Dad said.

"I'm not good enough in sports!" I said, my voice getting loud. "I'm not good enough in *anything*!"

"You *could* be—"

"No, Dad!" I yelled. "I'm not a super anything! I'm not a super student, I'm not a super athlete, I'm not a super musician! I'm not great at anything!"

"You don't *try*," he said.

Mom appeared around the side of the house. "Dennis, will you open the door for me, please? I left my key in my other bag."

"Just a minute," Dad said to me. "I'll be right back."

"I don't want to talk about this anymore," I said angrily. "I'm tired of arguing all the time!"

"You stay where you are," Dad said sternly. "I'm not finished with you yet."

He took his key out of the ignition and got out of the car.

I watched him walk up the driveway.

This will never end! I told myself. I'll never please him. He'll never be happy with me!

I threw myself back on the seat and kicked my foot at the dashboard.

But I missed the dashboard and hit the gear shift. I think the car started moving even before I knew what was happening.

The car rolled backward, down the driveway.

I looked quickly to see what was behind me.

And that's when I saw him.

Brian.

He was standing at the end of the driveway, with his hands in his pockets. He was looking across the street, away from me.

He didn't see the car heading right for him.

"Brian!" I screamed. "Brian! Move! Get out of the way! *BRIAN!*"

He couldn't hear me.

I flopped over and looked at the pedals on the floor of the car. One was to make the car go faster. One was the brake. I thought I knew which was which, but I wasn't sure.

I glanced back over my shoulder.

"No, God, don't let this happen!" I cried.

Something inside me screeched, *The horn! Honk the horn!*

I lunged at the horn and pushed it hard.

"Brian!" I screamed. *"Get out of the way!"*

Brian turned at the sound of the horn, but it was too late.

The car was right there.

He didn't have time to move.

The car knocked him down and ran over him. It was horrible, feeling the car go over a bump. A bump that was Brian.

The car finally stopped across the street, up in the neighbor's yard.

9

At the Hospital

The next few hours have blurry parts in my mind. I remember running in the house screaming "HELP!" and Brian's name over and over.

He lay in the driveway groaning and crying because he hurt so much.

Mom and Dad frantically ran back and forth between Brian and the telephone in the house.

I paced back and forth next to Brian. Please, God, please let Brian be okay, I whispered. I didn't mean those awful things I thought about him. I'm glad he's my brother! I love him. Please don't let anything happen to him.

The neighbors came over, asked if they could do anything, then stood around in the yard looking helpless.

The police came.

Then the ambulance came and took Brian away.

Dad, Mom, and I sped to the hospital as fast as the car would take us.

We waited in a reception area outside the emergency room for a long time. It could have been minutes, but it seemed like hours.

Dad and Mom didn't talk to each other or me. They sat like gray wooden statues, staring into space. I wished they would say something to break the silence. I wouldn't have minded if they had screamed at me.

The silence was awful.

I stared at the beige wallpaper and thought about Brian and all those things I'd thought about him. I wondered if God was punishing me for thinking terrible things about my own brother. Would God make Brian die just to teach me a lesson? Please, God, I prayed, please let Brian be all right. I've learned my lesson. Please take care of him. *Please.*

After a long time, the doctor came out and talked to my parents. I didn't understand all that she said, but it sounded as if Brian was in pretty bad shape.

His legs were broken. She thought his liver or spleen might have been injured, but she couldn't tell for sure without something called a CAT scan. And there was something about a fractured pelvis, but she didn't know for sure about that, either, without X-rays.

"May we see him?" my mom asked.

"You may see your son pretty soon," she said. "The orthopedist on call is on his way to the hospital. Brian is with a surgeon now. But as soon as the exam is over, you may go in and see him."

My parents asked more questions, and she answered the ones she could.

Then the doctor left and my parents went back to being statues.

The policeman that had come to the house appeared. He sat down on one of the vinyl-covered chairs in the corridor.

He took out a pad of paper and a pencil.

"Can you tell me what happened, folks?" he said, looking back and forth between my parents.

My dad looked at the cop with eyes that were glazed over.

"I know this is difficult for you," the policeman said, "but I need to make out a report."

Dad looked over at me.

"You want to tell him?" he said to me in a dull voice.

I sat up and swallowed hard. I tried to open my mouth, but it wouldn't work.

"That's all right, son," the policeman said in a soft voice. "Take your time."

I tried again. I took a big breath. "I—I was in the car," I said. Tears welled up in my eyes, but I didn't care who saw it. I didn't care about anything right then except Brian.

Please, God, make him be all right.

"Go on," the policeman said in a soft voice.

It was hard to make myself think about what I had done to my brother. It was even harder to *talk* about it. But I made myself do it.

"I was in the front seat. I was really mad." I looked at my dad and he looked away. I stopped and sniffed. My breathing started coming out in ragged gasps and I couldn't stop it. "I kicked at the dashboard. But I missed and hit the gear shift."

I put my head down and cried hard for a minute. I could feel my shoulders shaking with the crying. Finally, after the sobs were gone and I thought I could do it, I started talking again.

"The car started rolling backwards," I said, and then my voice got out of control and suddenly went really high. "I didn't know Brian was standing in the driveway! I tried to stop the car, I tried to yell at him, but he couldn't hear me." I felt very hot and kind of sick. "The car hit him, and it rolled—it rolled—"

Suddenly, everything went black.

I don't think I fainted longer than a few seconds because the policeman was moving toward me when I woke up with my head on the couch.

"You all right, son?" he said.

Mom rushed over to me. "Honey, are you okay?"

"Yeah," I said.

I tried to sit up, but Mom stopped me.

"Don't sit up yet," she said. She sat down beside me, and I put my head in her lap.

"I think I have enough for now," the policeman said. He closed his little notebook and slid it into his shirt pocket. "I'll be talking to you some more later." He nodded, and then he was gone.

Mom sat and stroked my head for awhile. I stared at the far end of the hallway, where a doorway opened onto another corridor.

Someone was walking toward me who looked familiar. I turned my head enough to see who it was.

It was Greg Madison.

He looked really out of it. Kind of scared and very sad. He came closer and just as he was about to pass, he looked over and saw me.

I didn't hold up my hand or smile, but I didn't look away either.

He looked as if he was going to say something to me. But then he must have decided not to.

He kept walking.

I lay there with my head on my mom's lap and wondered why Greg was here.

I didn't think about him very long, though. I went back to praying for Brian.

"Mr. and Mrs. Talbot?" It was the doctor again. "Would you all like to come in and see Brian? Then the surgeon would like to talk to you."

We jumped up and followed her into a room with lots of medical stuff standing around. In the middle of the room was Brian. He lay on a tall bed on wheels. A needle was stuck in his arm, and a tube ran from the needle up to a container hanging on a tall chrome stand on wheels.

Mom and Dad rushed over to him. I stood back a little. I wanted to talk to him, to tell him how sorry I was, but I didn't know if he'd want to talk to me. I didn't know if he could ever forgive me.

"Honey," Mom said, "are you okay? Are you in a lot of pain?"

Brian grimaced. "Yeah. The doctor gave me something for the pain. It's not as bad as it was."

Dad put a hand on Brian's arm. "She said you'd be all right, son," he said. "Thank God for that."

"Where's Justin?" Brian asked.

Dad and Mom turned silently to look at me. I walked over to Brian.

"Hi, Bri," I said.

"Hey, Sport," he said. His voice was weak. He tried to smile a little. "I'm getting a little sleepy." He nodded to the tube running from his arm. "The I.V."

I nodded, then I said, "Do you remember what happened?"

"The car hit me, right?" Brian said.

I started bawling again. "I'm sorry, Brian," I said. "I was mad and I kicked the gear shift and the car started rolling and—" A couple of loud sobs escaped then. "And I'm so sorry. I've been such a jerk to you—"

"Hey," Brian said softly. "Cut it out."

"No, you don't understand," I said.

How could I tell him about all the horrible things I'd thought about him? How could I apologize for thinking such terrible things about my own brother?

"Justin," Brian whispered in a weak voice. "You don't need to say anything more."

"Yes, I do—"

"Shut up and listen," he said.

I sniffed and nodded.

"I know what you've been going through," Brian said. "I should be apologizing to *you*—"

"*What?*" I cried.

"Just listen to me a minute," Brian said. "Ever since you were a little kid, everybody's compared you to me. I shouldn't have let that happen. That's not fair. We're not the same person. We have different talents and interests."

"But I've been mad at *you* about that," I said. "That wasn't right."

"That was a natural reaction," Brian said. "You don't have to walk in my footsteps. Don't even try. Make your own footsteps." He took hold of my hand. "Let God guide your direction."

I put my head down and buried my face in Brian's shoulder. "Brian," I said. "I was supposed to come in here to make *you* feel better."

Brian put a hand on my head.

"You're a great little brother, Justin," he said. "I'm very proud of you."

I straightened up. Dad came up behind me and squeezed my shoulder.

"I have two fine sons," he said quietly. He looked at Brian. "And I guess sometimes a father can learn a lot just listening to his sons. I think I need to do some thinking about what I've been doing to you, Justin. I can't tell you how sorry I am."

I put my arms around Dad and he hugged me really tight. Mom came over and hugged both my dad and me and then kissed Brian's cheek.

A nurse came in then and said she was going to take Brian upstairs.

"We'll see you later, son," Dad said.

"We'll be waiting," Mom said.

"Okay," Brian said.

I leaned down close to Brian's ear. "Thanks, Bri," I whispered. Then I said something I'd hadn't said since I was a little kid because it had seemed kind of sissy. "I love you."

It didn't seem sissy then. It felt like the right thing to say.

"I love you too," he whispered back. "See you later."

We watched the nurse wheel him away.

Thank You, God, I prayed. Thank You for my brother's life. Thank You for giving me Brian for a brother. I love him so much. Please help him.

10

Forgiveness

Brian stayed in the hospital for a couple of weeks. He had surgery that first night for a ruptured spleen, then he had both broken legs set and put in casts.

Mom stayed with him most of the time while he was in the hospital. I went over every day after school and visited him until it was suppertime. Dad spent the evenings with him. Arrangements were made with Brian's college so he could make up some of his work later in the semester. He started working on it during his last few days in the hospital.

It's a funny thing to say, but that time while Brian was at Mercy Hospital was a good time for all of us, even Brian. I could tell he thought so because he always looked so glad to see us. And Mandy. She came every day too. But I think Brian told her to come an hour later so that I could have time with him first.

Brian taught me how to play Backgammon, and we had some great Monopoly games.

And we talked.

Brian said I should really go after my interest in music.

"Really?" I said. "I didn't think you thought music was very important."

"I'm talking about *you*," he said. "Music is important to you. So go after it. Practice on your guitar. Get as good as you can."

"Yeah?"

"Yeah," Brian said. He smiled. "It'll make you happy. And besides, you're good at it. So with work, you'll get better."

"That'd be fun," I said.

"But you've got to study too," Brian said.

"I know."

"School has never been very hard for me," Brian said. "I've never really had to study as hard as some kids. Math and science come pretty easy for me."

I rolled my eyes. "Those are my hardest subjects," I said.

"For you, maybe," Brian said. "English is my bad subject."

"It's my favorite!" I said. "After music."

"See?" Brian said. "We just have different talents."

"Yeah," I said. "I guess you're right."

One day during the last week that Brian was in the hospital, I was walking down the corridor, and I saw Greg Madison again. He got off the elevator and walked toward me.

I couldn't really avoid him; there was nowhere I could go except backward. And that would've looked pretty stupid.

"Hi," he said and slowed as we got close to each other.

"Hi," I said.

"I heard about your brother," Greg said.

I nodded. "Who are you here to see?"

"My dad," Greg said. "He had an accident on his motorcycle."

"Oh," I said. I felt self-conscious and pulled on my ear. "Sorry."

"He almost died," Greg said.

I folded my arms in front of me and nodded.

"Oh," Greg said. He reached into his deep jacket pocket, and when his hand came out, it was holding my CD. The one he had stolen from me.

He handed it to me. "This is yours," he said. "I guess you left it at my house after all."

I was so surprised, I didn't know what to say. I took the CD.

"Thanks," I said finally.

He shrugged. "I thought I'd bump into you one of these days with your brother here and all."

His eyes met mine, and in a split second, something really weird happened. There was something in his eyes that made us like brothers. He had gone through a lot while his dad was in the hospital, I guess. The look in his eyes said that he knew about my pain too. I think that's why he gave me the CD back.

He hadn't admitted that he had stolen it from me. And he hadn't said he was sorry for chasing me off that day.

But he didn't need to. I knew he was sorry.

That was enough.

I watched him walk away from me down the hall.

Right then and there, I forgave Greg in my mind for stealing from me. It felt awfully good to get that out of my system. I think God took the bad feelings from me as soon as He helped me forgive Greg.

It felt as good to forgive Greg as it had felt being forgiven by Brian.

And speaking of forgiveness, after my dad told me he was sorry that first day in the emergency room, things between us got better too.

He stopped pushing me so hard to be a great athlete. He even stopped the training sessions for awhile.

But you know what? I kind of missed them. So I asked him if he'd just come to the track once in a while to give me some pointers.

He said he'd be glad to.

Now I run for the fun of it. It sure makes it more enjoyable not to have to try and be a star every time I run. And since I'm enjoying it more, I'm running better than ever.

But Dad seems happy when I *do* my best now. I don't have to *be* the best any more.

One day, a couple of weeks after Brian was out of the hospital, Dad took me out for breakfast. Just the two of us.

Over blueberry pancakes he told me he was proud of me.

"You don't have to earn that from me," Dad said. "I'm proud of you just because you're my son."

"Thanks, Dad," I said.

It was terrific to hear him say it. But we were out in public, so I was hoping this wouldn't get mushy. I glanced over my shoulder, but no one seemed to be listening at any of the nearby tables.

"You know," he said, "ever since you and Brian were little boys, I've prayed for you guys. I wanted the best for both of you. I want you to achieve and do well and be happy."

"I know, Dad," I said.

"But Brian made me realize that I was praying for the wrong things," he said. "I was praying for you to excel in the ways *I* thought you should."

I nodded.

He took a big bite of his pancakes and chewed thoughtfully.

"I think," he said after swallowing them, "that I should leave you in God's care now. I know that God loves you, as I do. I'll guide you with family matters and house rules as always. But I think I'll let God shape your future. I know you'll follow in the way He directs you."

"I'll try," I said.

Dad sipped some coffee. Then he set his cup down on the table. "And who knows? Maybe God *wants* you to pursue your music. You love it so much. Maybe He's been gently tugging at your arm to go that way."

"Maybe." I really didn't know whether my love of music had anything to do with God tugging at me or not. But I had a feeling that God had a lot to do with this conversation I was having with my dad.

"I have a surprise for you," Dad said.

"A surprise?"

He reached into his pocket and brought out a little slip of paper. He slid it across the table to me.

On the paper was a name I didn't recognize and a telephone number. I looked up at my dad. "What's this?"

"Your new guitar teacher," said Dad.

"What?"

He was smiling from ear to ear. "I called Paul Bixby's dad and got the name of a very good teacher here in town. His name is George Hanson. Mr. Bixby says he's the best. I called Hanson and he's agreed to take you as a student. Money's pretty tight right now, so the lessons will be every other week."

I was absolutely speechless. "Dad, I—I—" I shook my head while I stammered. "This is—just—just—"

"—great?" my dad said. He was laughing.

"No," I said. "*STUPENDOUS!*"

My dad laughed some more.

"Thanks, Dad," I said. "Thanks a whole lot."

"You bet, son."

I'm in sixth grade now, and all of this seems very far away. Brian is back to normal, and so am I.

But normal is better now. My dad and I don't always agree on everything, but we get along better. I'm studying harder, getting better grades, and running for fun. I think I'll join the track team next year in junior high.

And I'm getting really good on my guitar. Mr. Hanson says I'm one of the best students he's ever had. Not because of raw talent, he says, but because I work hard at it. And because I love it.

There's that word again. Love. I said it to Brian that day in the hospital, and he said it back. And I know I feel it more for everybody in my family. I think that must be God's best gift to us all.

Because He loves us, we can love one another. And because He forgives us, we can forgive one another.

And I think that's what life on earth and in heaven is all about.